Tales of Victorian Sheffield

No. 3

OUTRAGE!

The Story of William Broadhead and the Trade Union Scandals of Victorian Sheffield

told by
Peter Machan

Note to teachers.

This book has been designed to support the requirements of the National Literacy Strategy. It fits in well with the Year 6, Term 1 work on non-fiction, biography, and links with a study of Victorian England.

© Peter Machan 2001

Printed and published by:
ALD Design & Print
279 Sharrow Vale Road
Sheffield S11 8ZF

Telephone: 0114 267 9402
Email: a.lofthouse@btinternet.com

ISBN 1-901587-14-2

First Published 2001

Other titles in the series

The Fantastic Career of Charlie Peace 1832 - 1879,
  A True Tale of Victorian Villainy - Peter Machan   *ISBN 1-901587-08-8*

The Sheffield Flood, 11th March 1864 - Peter Machan   *ISBN 1-901587-13-4*

Contents

Chapter		Page
Introduction	The Name on the Blade	v
1	Outrage!	1
2	The Shooting of Elisha Parker	6
3	The Acorn Street Explosion	11
4	Downfall of the Grinder King	15

William Broadhead, 'The Grinder King'
Secretary of the Saw Grinders' Union and
Publican of *The Royal George* public house, Calver Street.

Introduction

The Name on the Blade

Whenever anyone in the mid-nineteenth century, in countries all around the globe, reached out for a tool to cut with, they were almost certain to read the name of the town of Sheffield on the blade. It could be the tailor reaching for his scissors, the Australian farmer shearing his sheep, the Indian soldier having his morning shave, the butcher carving a joint of meat, the American cowboy dusting off his Bowie knife, the Irish labourer scything through the ripe corn or the gentleman sitting down to his breakfast table. Sheffield was famous the world over for producing blades of every sort.

Not so famous, however, were the thousands of men and women who toiled in the hundreds of mills, factories and workshops to shape the steel bars into the blades and then to make their edges sharp and put handles of every description onto them. It was the forgers who hammered the hot steel bars into shape on an anvil, the grinders who finished the shape off and put on the sharp edge by holding the blade against a spinning grindstone and the cutlers who fitted the handles.

The work was dirty and dangerous, especially for the grinders who would constantly breathe in the deadly mixture of sandstone particles and tiny fragments of steel which would eventually kill them. Sheffield was a working town and was not ashamed of the great black clouds of smoke which belched from the forest of factory chimneys. Most people were poor and were glad of any work they could get. Thousands flocked to the growing town every year to find jobs. So, even though Sheffield was as busy as could be, there were never enough jobs for everyone.

It was only natural that the men in work would want to protect their jobs. It was understandable that they would wish to make rules to keep out outsiders, who might work for less pay. And it was understandable that they should have got together in trades unions to try to stop the factory owners from taking advantage of them. But some people went just too far.

This is the fascinating story of one man, William Broadhead, who took the law into his own hands and used his authority over his trade union to rule by means of intimidation, threats, violence and, ultimately, by murder.

Chapter 1

OUTRAGE!

It was April 5th of the year 1867, and the Speaker of the House of Commons was about to call the Home Secretary to make an announcement to Parliament regarding the appalling series of attacks, shootings, explosions and murders which had taken place in the town of Sheffield. The whole country had recently been shocked by the graphic newspaper accounts of these events, for William Leng, the campaigning new editor of the local paper, *The Sheffield Daily Telegraph*, had made it his personal mission to throw light on the threateningly dark and murky tactics used by various of the town's trades unions to maintain their authority.

The final event which had led to today's announcement in Parliament had been a gunpowder explosion which had rocked the town centre at five o'clock one morning in the previous October, destroying most of the home of Thomas Fernehough in Hereford Street. Miraculously, none of the sleeping family were seriously injured. It did not take William Leng long to establish that Fernehough, a saw grinder, had made himself extremely unpopular with the Saw Handle Makers Union for working while their members were on strike. The grinder even showed Leng a number of anonymous letters which he had received threatening that he would be shot if he carried on. Leng was quite sure that the finger of guilt pointed to one particularly unscrupulous man, William Broadhead, the Secretary of the Saw Grinders' Union, but such was the web of fear which he spun around himself that no-one could be persuaded, even when a reward of two thousand pounds was offered, to come forward and give evidence against Broadhead.

The sweeping legal powers which Walpole, the Home Secretary, was about to grant to his Commissioners, however, would ensure that witnesses had no choice but to come forward. Such powers were quite without parallel in English legal history, either before or since. Such was the gravity with which Parliament viewed the worsening situation in the rapidly-expanding northern industrial town.

"Order! This House will come to order! The House calls The Home Secretary, Mr. Walpole."

"Mr. Speaker, I have become increasingly disturbed by the continuing reports of threats, violence and intimidation which I have received from the town of Sheffield. Mr. Leng and the proprietors of the Sheffield Daily Telegraph have presented to me evidence of over two hundred such cases which have occurred as a result of disputes between trades unions in the various branches of the tool and cutlery trades. There are indeed indications that these cowardly groups have not stopped at acts of violence, but have committed murder itself, and that responsibility for the atrocities recently committed in that town are part of a conspiracy.

I put it to the house that it is a most dangerous and appalling situation that these despicable groups should interfere with the free

2

regulation of trade and threaten the lives and livelihoods of honest working people.

I therefore present to the house a Bill to set up a Commission of Inquiry to establish the facts behind these outrages in Sheffield and to bring those responsible to justice. In order for the truth to be found the Commission should have the power to enforce attendance on any person that it calls to give evidence and to grant certificates of indemnity to those who confess their part in these crimes."

News that the Act to establish 'The Commission of Inquiry into the Sheffield Trade Outrages' had been passed was greeted back in the town in various ways. None welcomed the news more than William Leng, the campaigning editor of the *Telegraph.* He wasted no time in calling on the Chief Constable, John Jackson to share the excellent news, though the police chief expressed some reservations regarding the unprecedented powers given to the Commission.

"You've heard the wonderful news, Mr. Jackson? They passed the Bill in Parliament this morning to open a Commission of Inquiry into the trade outrages."

"Yes I have just received a telegraph message about it. I must say it's typical that you newspaper fellows found out before I did myself! But did you hear that the Home Secretary has granted free pardons to all those who give evidence, whatever their crime?"

William Leng, Editor of
The Sheffield Daily Telegraph

"Yes, indeed. Now we should be able to break through the fear that has forced all the victims to keep silent up to now."

"I'm sure that you're right, but I can't say that I'm happy with the whole idea of letting criminals go unpunished."

"Oh, come now, Mr. Jackson, at last we should be able to bring down that swaggering villain Broadhead that everyone knows is behind it all."

William Broadhead, the subject of the conversation, put on a public show of indifference to the investigations of the proposed commissioners and even went so far as to say that he also welcomed the Commission and of condemning all those involved in violence and intimidation. He had even contributed to a reward, to be offered to anyone coming forward with information regarding the recent bomb attack on the home of Fernehough. That was typical of the bluff and domineering Broadhead, who revelled in his nickname of 'Owd Smeet'em'. It was commonly understood that he would stop at nothing to protect the interests of his members, and the many other union leaders in Sheffield looked to him for advice.

John Jackson
Chief Constable of Sheffield

Under his iron grip the Saw Grinders' Union had become the most efficient and powerful of the dozens in the Sheffield cutlery and tool trades. Broadhead held an undisputed position of power in the town and he was unwilling to admit that anything could loosen his

4

grip on the reins. He delighted in his fierce reputation and few dared to speak against him at the weekly union meetings at the Royal George public house on Calver Street, where Broadhead was the landlord.

"I'll not have it, I tell you Hallam. And our members won't have it either. That man Leng using the pages of his wretched paper to blacken my good character. I believe that their statements are libellous and I intend to

The Royal George, now demolished

take legal proceedings to stop it. He's a damned fool poking his nose into affairs that he doesn't understand."

"But what about this Commission of Inquiry, Mr. Broadhead? It looks to me as if they are out to get us!"

"Don't you let me hear you talking like that", thundered Broadhead, beating his great fist down onto the polished bar counter. "Everything we've done has been to protect our members, don't you forget it. There's no reason why they should turn against us now. You just let me know if you hear of anybody that's going to talk out of turn. We know how to deal with them!"

James Hallam nodded and sipped his beer nervously. He was one of those who knew only too well how the overbearing landlord dealt with those who opposed him.

Chapter 2

The Shooting of Elisha Parker

The Royal Commission sat in June 1859 under William Overend in the Town Hall Council Chamber and began to look into the 209 cases of violence and intimidation which had been collected by the press, police and the manufacturers. Throughout the next five weeks a complicated and frightening story of intimidation, bullying, violence and murder was gradually dragged from a series of unwilling and terrified witnesses. Gradually one man's was name was to emerge at the centre of the web of intrigue, especially when the police's main witness, James Hallam, under promise of a free pardon, tremblingly and sobbingly admitted his own part in a number of atrocities and implicated William Broadhead, *'The Grinder King'*. Details of the crimes, as they began to unfold, were reported in the national newspapers, and shocked the whole country.

The first few days of the hearing were uneventful enough and it began to appear to those few who attended that William Broadhead's swaggering self-confidence had been justified. The court heard witnesses recount details of events which had taken place over the previous ten years and which were well enough known to the locals who packed the courtroom from newspaper reports. Nevertheless, the stories they had to tell, such as that told by Elisha Parker on the fifth day of the Inquiry were frightful enough to shock the Commissioners.

"Please state your name and position," began William Overend as the first witness took his position.*

"I am Elisha Parker and I am the postmaster at Dore village where I also have a smallholding".

"But it was not this which brought you so much unwelcome attention from the unions, was it Mr. Parker?"

"Indeed not, your honour. I was at that time also working as a saw grinder."

"And where was that, Mr. Parker?"

"I was working at Samuel Newbould's, that's Bridgefield Works on Sheffield Moor.'

"And can you please tell us the circumstances that led up to your terrible injuries?"

"Well, as far as I can remember, it all started to get nasty when I

was woken up one night by William Broadhead and another man beating on the door. They said that there had been a meeting that night and that I was to stop working immediately."

"When was this?"

"This would be in June 1854."

"And why did the union wish you to stop working?"

"Well, there had been a dispute between Mr. Newbould and the union for some time and the men had been out on strike for months. I couldn't see the point myself, and when I was offered the job at a good rate I was pleased to have it."

"So did you agree to stop working as Mr. Broadhead asked?"

"No I didn't. I told them I wouldn't. They argued and threatened me, saying I was damaging the power of the union, but I told them I couldn't afford to cease the work."

"So what happened as a result of this?"

"It was one morning about a month later when I went up the lane to collect my horse from the field beside the Door Moor Inn to ride to work when I heard a terrible wailing and snorting noise from the animal. When I got there it was in a terrible state. Somebody had hamstrung it in the night and the poor thing was bleeding terribly. It had to be put down."

"And did you suspect that this incident was related to the threats?"

"I was sure it was. In fact I went back to Broadhead and I told him I wouldn't pay any more union money until he'd paid me £20 for the loss of the horse."

"It was then that things took a more serious turn, was it not?"

"It certainly was. One night in the following March I had ridden home through driving rain and I was tired out so when I'd had supper I went straight to bed. Fortunately for us my wife's mother was still up drying the wet clothes in front of the fire when she heard a noise outside the door. When she opened the door into the yard she got the shock of her life! There was a man laid on the step pushing gunpowder under the door! She screamed and rushed up to warn us but before we got down the stairs there was an explosion that threw us off our feet. It caused considerable damage to the back of the house and shook us all up badly but no one was badly hurt."

"I believe that you started to take precautions to protect yourself after that."

"I did. I bought a shotgun and a large dog and I had strong shutters fitted to all the windows."

"But this did not prevent a further attack on you, I understand?"

"No sir, it did not. It was one night the following June, at Whitsuntide when we'd been really busy. I was dozing in my chair by the fire when I heard someone throw a handful of stones onto the roof. I reached for my gun and waited. It happened again so I quietly unbolted the back door and looked out and called. There was nothing to be seen so I walked across the yard to look at the roof. It was then that there was a flash and the crack of gunfire from behind the hedge across the lane. I turned quickly and saw another flash further down the lane and felt a sharp pain in my right arm. I staggered into the middle of the lane and saw a man's head raise from behind the hedge. I wasn't going to let them get away lightly so I raised the gun to my shoulder but before I could fire I was thrown backwards by the force of pellets shot into my arm and neck. All I remember after that is one of my neighbours carrying me back to the house and the vicar being sent for. He insisted that I should go straight to the General Infirmary. They wanted to take my arm off, but I wouldn't let them. It was eleven

9

weeks before I was well enough to go back home. "

"And I believe that you were unable to work for a considerable length of time following this? "

"Yes sir. It was a full year before I was fit for work again. "

Table Knife Grinders, 1912
Notice how the sleeves have been cut from their jackets
to avoid them being caught on the grindstone.

Chapter 3

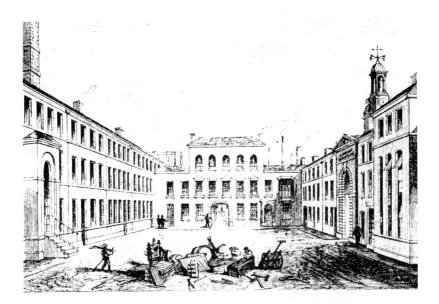

The Acorn Street Explosion

As a succession of such witnesses gave their evidence it soon became clear that any employer who had taken on non-union labour or had broken one of the unions many newly-written rules was likely to find themselves receiving the unwelcome attention of the unions' bully boy enforcers, as were those workers who fell in arrears with their union dues, or 'natty money'. The threats generally started with a warning note, anonymous but frequently signed 'Mary Ann'. No-one in the trade had any doubts who Mary Ann was. If this warning was not heeded the workplace may be 'rattened', that is the men's tools taken or the leather belts which drove the grinding wheels cut or stolen and the damage blamed on the rats. Generally this brought success and the victim of the action would pay up the overdue dues as well as a charge levied to compensate the union for the trouble it had taken to collect the overdue amount.

As shocking as the shooting of Elisha Parker was, the Commissioners were to hear stories of other brutal attacks which had ended far more tragically. Neither was it always the intended target who became the victim. Such was the shocking case of Mrs. O'Rourke, a woman who kept a lodging house on Acorn Street, near Kelham Island, almost opposite the imposing gateway to Green Lane Works, Henry Hoole's stove grate factory. It was as a result of a trade dispute at this works that the unfortunate Irish lady was killed. The target, however, was her lodger.

From the early months of 1861 the fender grinders at Hoole's had been on strike. Henry Hoole took a typically brusque and uncompromising attitude towards the dispute and hired several new grinders, non-union men. One of these was George Wastnage, an out of work grinder from Mexbrough. Hoole's union officials met with

Gateway of Green Lane Works, Henry Hoole's stove grate works The gateway still stands today

William Broadhead for advice on how to deal with the situation. It was agreed to try persuasion first and so a meeting was arranged between Broadhead and the officials of the Fender Grinders Union and the non-union workers at a local pub. Over a pint of ale the strikers tried to bribe Wastnage and the others to leave. They refused, conscious of the fact that work was very difficult to find. Wastnage, however, offered to join the union. His offer was turned down.

Later that same night, in the small hours of the morning, the Wastnages and their small son lay asleep in their attic bedroom when they, and their landlady, Bridget O'Rourke, asleep in the room below, were suddenly startled awake by the shattering of a bedroom window. A parcel, wrapped in brown paper, lay hissing and sparking beside the Irishwoman's bed. Harriet Wastnage, hearing fleeing footsteps, peered out of her window onto the dim cobbled street below, before racing down the stairs to see what was amiss. She was later to recount the story of her terrible ordeal that night to the Commissioners.

"When you looked out of your window, what did you see?" began William Overend.

"I saw a lot of men running down the street, three or four."

"And when you went to Mrs. O'Rourke's chamber, what did you see?"

"I saw Mrs. O'Rourke standing in the corner against her bed. I told her to throw it out of the window."

"To throw what?"

"Why, the parcel that was blazing. Sparks were flying out."

"What happened next?"

"She wouldn't touch it so I snatched it up myself to throw it out but it went off in my hand."

"And did you become immediately insensible?"

"Of course. It went off!" snapped Mrs, Wastnage.

"You do not recollect anything more until you found yourself in the Infirmary?"

"No I do not. I was very much burned and blinded."

"Do you still feel any injury from that time now?"

"Yes I do. My right eye fails me badly and I have no use of my right hand."

"How long were you blind?"

"About a fortnight."

It was probably as well that Harriet Wastnage had been spared the memory of that terrible night, for her husband reported that she had suffered such frightful burns that, screaming in pain, she had pulled away from him as he tried to tear off her burning clothes and had fallen from the window into the street. Even so, she was more fortunate than their landlady, who was discovered, for some reason, in the cellar, laying unconscious, her body blackened. She never recovered consciousness, but died from the burns in hospital two weeks later.

A ruffian called Robert Renshaw was now called to give evidence of his part in this attack. After much evasion, lying and bluster, Renshaw, on the promise of a free pardon, finally admitted that he had indeed been one of the shadowy figures that Harriet Wastnage had spotted fleeing from the scene of crime six years previously, and that he had been paid six pounds by officials of the Fender Grinders union to commit the brutal attack.

Chapter 4

A Blade Forging Shop

Downfall of the Grinder King

It was on the seventh day of the Inquiry that James Hallam was called to give evidence. Until this point the evidence, though shocking, had revealed little that had not already appeared in the press. Hallam, however, was the key witness on whom both Leng and the police were relying to finally implicate the unions, and particularly William Broadhead as Secretary of the Saw Grinders Union, in the outrages. Hallam had already been questioned by the chief constable and, in fear of his life, had made a private statement about his part in a number of unsolved incidents. He now stood before the court; a thin-faced, weasely and shifty-looking character, visibly nervous, casting occasional uncomfortable glances across at Broadhead, who fixed him with a steely gaze.

15

Mr. Overend opened with a line of questioning regarding Hallam's part in the rattening of a cutlery firm called Taylor's. This revealed no facts that were not already well enough known, though Hallam's answers were to reveal just how unscrupulous a man this was.

"James Hallam, You know Broadhead I suppose?"

"Yes."

"Has he ever paid you to do business for him?"

"No."

"Speak the truth. The law is strong enough to protect you from violence if you tell the truth."

"I might have asked him if he had any jobs for me."

"Do you know of Mathew Broadhead and Samuel Hallam who worked for Taylor's?"

"I do."

"Did you take the nuts from their grinding wheels so that they could not work?"

"Yes. They were in arrears with their natty money."

"And did they pay up after you had taken the nuts?"

"I believe they did."

"Did you get any money for doing this job?"

"Yes, 25 shillings."

"Who paid you?"

16

"I can't tell you his name."

"Did you talk to Broadhead about the job?"

"No, I believe I never."

"Who was Sam Hallam, was he your father?"

"He was my father."

The Grinding Room

The questioning then turned to the incident at Wheatman and Smith's, a saw grinding firm on Kelham Island, which had attracted the unwelcome attention of union enforcers when they planned to introduce new machinery for grinding saws, for the union took the view that this was a threat to jobs. In January 1860, late one Saturday night, a large charge of explosives had been pushed up a drainpipe leading into the factory and the resulting explosion had caused extensive damage to the works. When asked about his part in the affair, Hallam became distinctly uncooperative, even though he had previously admitted his involvement to John Jackson.

"Had Wheatman and Smith's a kind of machine which would grind saws?"

"Not that I know of."

"Did you ever try to blow up their premises?"

"No."

"Did you buy gunpowder for this purpose?"

"No."

"Did you ever put gunpowder at the bottom of their chimney?"

"No."

"Did you go to Broadhead on the following Saturday and did he give you £15 in sovereigns for the job?"

"No."

"I will warn you again that if you don't tell us the truth you will be indicted for lying. Did you make a full statement of your part in blowing up Wheatmen's to Mr. Jackson the Chief Constable?"

"It was a false statement."

"Did you not give a detailed description of how you came to do it?"

"Very likely I did."

"You made up the story?"

"I did."

"Who put it into your head to invent such a story?"

"Nobody."

"Did you tell Mr. Jackson you were afraid for your life?"

"Very likely I did."

"Are you afraid of speaking out now?"

"I would rather go on as we are doing."

"You have told us that you were responsible for the rattening at Taylor's. Who was with you?"

"I will not tell you."

"If you continue to refuse to answer in a truthful way I must send you to prison. Call a policeman to take Mr. Hallam into custody. James Hallam we sentence you to six weeks in Wakefield House of Correction for contempt of court."

Prison life, however, was not to Hallam's liking and only five days later he was back in front of Mr. Overend in a distinctly more talkative mood.

"The last time you were here you refused to tell us who was with you when you rattened Taylor. Will you tell us now?"

"Yes, It was Sam Crooks."

"And did you both go to Broadhead?"

"Yes."

"And did you receive any money from him?"

"Yes."

The questioning now turned to the Wheatman's incident.

"Were you ever at Wheatman's?"

"Yes."

"Who planned it with you?"

"Crooks."

"What did he tell you?"

"He said we had a job to do, to blow it up."

"And did Broadhead give you any money?"

"Yes, £2."

"What was the money for?"

"To buy gunpowder."

"And after you had blown up the works did you see Broadhead again?"

"Yes, we saw him at his own house."

"What did he say?"

"He said it would do very well."

The mood in the courtroom was now tense. Until this point Broadhead had observed the proceedings in an aloof and condescending manner. He had been called to give evidence already but had consistently denied any part in initiating threats or violence, and had maintained a slightly aggrieved attitude that his word should be questioned. Unsure glances were now exchanged around the packed room between the many who wondered which direction the Commissioner's questioning was now leading. Overend no longer hesitated but pressed his advantage by unexpectedly moving his questioning to Hallam's part in the murder of James Linley.

Linley had made himself an extremely unpopular figure in the trade. He had set himself up as a saw grinder without a proper apprenticeship to do so and had repeatedly taken on apprentices to work for him at cheap rates and then put them out of work as soon as they were eligible for full pay. This flooded the trade with cheap labour and undercut the union rates. To make matters worse Linley made no secret of his disdain for the union and could be seen drinking heavily in front of men who had not got the price of a pint. He had been shot and wounded in the side through a window in a friend's house in November 1857, and some time later he escaped a further attempt on his life when a bomb shattered his brother-in - law's shop in the Wicker where he was staying. In February 1860, however, Linley's luck ran out. Whilst sitting drinking in the snug of the *Crown Inn* on Scotland Street a shot shattered the window and hit him in the side of the head. He was carried to Mr. Booth's surgery in Paradise Square but the doctor could do little and Linley died a few weeks later.

"Do you recollect the time when Linley was shot?"

"Yes."

"On the Saturday night before were you seen in Wilson's bar in West Street with a pistol in your pocket?"

"Yes."

"Where did you get it from?"

"I bought it."

"For what purpose?"

Hallam hung his head. His breathing came heavily. Clearly he was extremely uncomfortable with this turn of questioning. He didn't answer immediately.

"I ask you again for what purpose you bought the pistol?"

Still Hallam hesitated and grew increasingly agitated. Overend became insistent to the point of impatience.

"Answer the Question!"

"I shall answer only if I may have my Certificate."

"You shall have it, as may any other witnesses who are prepared to come forward and tell the truth."

But the pressure of the questioning and the horror of catching Broadhead's piercing eyes across the courtroom were too much for Hallam. With a whimper his knees buckled and he fainted onto the floor. He was supported from the room. Once outside he revived a little but would only consent to return to give evidence on condition that the Chief Constable sat between Broadhead and himself so that he could not see his eyes. Once these arrangements had been made questioning resumed in the hushed and expectant room.

"Why did you buy the pistol?"

"To shoot Linley."

"Was there anyone else involved in the shooting?"

"Yes, Samuel Crookes."

"Who shot him?"

"I compelled Crookes to do it."

22

"What did he shoot him with?"

"An air gun."

"Had any person set you up to do anything to Linley?'

"I had asked Broadhead one day what he was going to do about Linley."

"And what did he say?"

"He asked me what I could do for him."

"And what did you say?"

"I told him I could make him as he would not work any more."

"What did he say to that?"

"He asked me what I should want for doing it."

"What did you say?"

"I asked him if £20 would be too much."

"And what did he say to that?"

"He said no, he should think not."

The courtroom was now in uproar. Leng looked up from his feverish scribbling in his reporter's notebook to cast a knowing look of satisfaction towards John Jackson. The chairman's gavel hammered hard down again and again on the table until eventually the mutterings and murmurings, amongst which the name of William Broadhead could be picked out distinctly, began to subside into a quiet rumble. The proceedings were adjourned and Hallam was released from the morning's ordeal.

23

For the afternoon session the court was packed with a noisy and excited audience anticipating fresh revelations. They were not to be disappointed for William Overend now called Samuel Crookes to give evidence.

"Do you know that James Hallam was here this morning and has made serious charges against you?"

"Yes."

"He says that he and you were employed by Broadhead to do injury to Linley, that you had an airgun and had followed Linley from place to place for five or six weeks. Is that true?"

"Yes."

"He also says that having been paid £20 by Broadhead you followed him to a public house in Scotland Street where you shot him in the head. If you are guilty we are able to grant you a certificate that would protect you from the consequences of your admission. Can you make a clean breast of it?"

"Yes, I did it."

"Who first suggested doing the job, was it Broadhead?"

"Yes, I think it was."

"How was Linley doing you an injury?"

"He was setting a whole lot of lads on, filling the trade and spoiling things altogether."

"Did Broadhead agree to give you money?"

"Yes."

"And what did you agree to do for him?"

"We only agreed to do something to Linley. We didn't mean to kill him but there was a lot of people in the room. I couldn't get a clear shot. I tried to hit him in the shoulder but he bent forward and I hit him in the head."

"If you have told the truth you will get your certificate."

"Well, I hope I shall, but my character's gone, I am sorry to say."

"Never mind that. We have nothing to do with that. We cannot talk about the character of a man who has committed crimes like yours."

"It is a bad one. I am ashamed of it."

William Broadhead was called back to the dock. Although he continued to maintain his aloof air he could do little to deny that he had indeed hired Crookes and Hallam to shoot Linley.

"What justification could you have for taking such action?" asked William Overend.

"I had every right to take these actions since the law does not protect the working man. If the law would give the unions some power then we should not have to resort to such measures and such things would never be heard of again."

There were many who shared Brodhead's views, but he had lost his power and influence. He needed to be escorted by the police from the courtroom, through the jeering crowds which now blocked the way to his carriage. Soon after this the magistrates refused to renew the licence of *The Royal George*. There was nothing left for Broadhead in Sheffield so, with the help of cash from a fund set up by supporters, he set off to start a new life in America.

John Jackson was awarded a silver salver and a cheque for six hundred pounds from the grateful townspeople. William Leng got a knighthood and six hundred guineas.

Life in America did not suit Broadhead, and he soon returned to Sheffield, where he took a grocer's shop on Meadow Street. He died in 1878 and was buried without ceremony in Ecclesall churchyard.

Finishing Knife Handles